STORY OF
THE CHRISTMAS ROSE

Retold by
I.M. Richardson
Illustrated by
Kees deKiefte

Troll Associates

Library of Congress Cataloging in Publication Data

Richardson, I.M.
    Story of the Christmas rose.

    Summary: A boy's kindness to two small animals one
snowy Christmas Eve results in his discovery of the
fabled Christmas rose, bringing magical joy to him and
his family.
    [1. Fairy tales. 2. Folklore—Norway. 3. Christmas—
Folklore] I. Kiefte, Kees de, ill. II. Title.
PZ8.R3923St   1988   398.2 '36 [E]   87-1381
    ISBN 0-8167-1069-4 (lib. bdg.)
    ISBN 0-8167-1070-8 (pbk.)

Copyright © 1988 by Troll Associates, Mahwah, N.J.

STORY OF
THE CHRISTMAS ROSE

No one could be certain there was a Christmas rose. No one had ever seen it, yet people still talked about it. They said it grew in the deep snow on the side of the mountain. They said the only person who would ever be able to find it would have to be good and kind and brave.

The young woodcutters laughed at the idea, for they had never seen a red rose growing in the snow. The old driver of the coach had never seen it either, in all the years he had been riding over the mountain.

Finally the king himself decided to settle the matter once and for all. So one Christmas he went out in his sleigh to look for the Christmas rose. He brought hundreds of servants with him, and they traveled over every inch of the mountain. But they could not find the Christmas rose.

Then the townspeople said, "If the king cannot find the Christmas rose, then surely it does not exist."

Now it happened that a tiny cottage sat at the foot of the mountain. A poor woodcutter lived in the cottage with his wife and two children, a boy and a girl.

The woodcutter had broken his leg, and he could not work. His wife was so sick that she could not even get out of bed. And although tomorrow was Christmas day, there was no money to buy a Christmas tree.

"It will not seem like Christmas without a tree," said the girl.

"I know," replied the boy. He put on his coat and hat. "I will go to the top of the mountain and cut down a tree," he said. "You stay here and keep the fire burning." Then he pulled on his boots and went outside.

The cold wind dug its icy fingers right through the
boy's coat. His nose and fingers felt as if they were made
of icicles. But he pushed on through the snow, shifting
his ax from one shoulder to the other. As he walked, he
hummed a little tune to keep himself company.

   As the sun dropped lower in the sky, dark shadows reached out toward the boy, and he became afraid. He looked up at the huge evergreen trees towering above him. They were all too big to cut, so he climbed farther up the mountain.

Before long he came upon a little rabbit whose foot was caught in a trap. The rabbit was struggling to get free, and the more he struggled, the tighter the trap squeezed his foot. The boy knew he would have to hurry if he was going to find a tree and be home before dark, but he stopped to help the rabbit.

His fingers were so stiff from the cold that he could hardly move them, but he kept on trying. Finally he was able to set the rabbit free.

"Thank you," cried the rabbit. "Merry Christmas!" And he scampered off.

The boy smiled and moved up the mountain. Now
the snow was so deep that he slipped and stumbled again
and again. By and by he happened upon a tiny field
mouse, who was nearly buried in the snow.

"He looks starved," thought the boy, picking up the mouse and warming him with his breath. "Maybe I can find something for him to eat." And with that, he began looking around in the snow.

Before long he found a few berries underneath a huge pine tree. The mouse ate as if he were at a banquet and then jumped down. "Thank you," he called. "Merry Christmas!" And then he scampered away.

By this time, the boy's feet were nearly frozen. He started out again, but the snow was so deep that he had to move very slowly. With each step, he grew more and more tired. Finally he was so exhausted that he had to sit down on a tree stump to catch his breath.

The sun had set, and the mountainside was in darkness. The boy realized that he would not be able to find a Christmas tree now. He thought of how disappointed his sister would be, and two tiny tears ran down his cheeks. As they fell into the snow, something wonderful happened.

The forest suddenly grew brighter, and the mountainside was bathed in a warm, red glow. The boy looked up and saw that a lovely green rosebush had appeared directly in front of him.

At the very top of the bush was a single red rose, more beautiful than any he had ever seen. Its petals glistened and seemed to shine like rubies.

He carefully reached out and picked the rose. The rosebush disappeared, and darkness again fell on the forest. But the light from the rose was like a glowing torch in his hand, showing him the way safely down the mountainside.

As the boy passed through the village, people could
hardly believe their eyes.

"Look! Look!" they whispered. "It's the Christmas rose! A child has found the Christmas rose!" Then the shopkeepers came out of their shops to gaze in wonder at the sight.

When the boy arrived home, he said to his sister, "I could not find a Christmas tree, but look! I found this flower in the snow." The light from the Christmas rose spread out into the darkest corners of the room.

As the light touched the children's father, he jumped up as if his leg had never been broken. "The Christmas rose!" he said.

And as the light touched the children's mother, she sat up in bed as if she were in perfect health. "The Christmas rose!" she exclaimed.

The girl's eyes grew wide with wonder. "Oh!" she said. "It is so beautiful!"

Then there came a gentle knocking at the door, as if someone did not want to intrude. The girl lifted the latch and opened the door. There in the snow stood the king, his golden crown shining and his jewels sparkling. But they seemed dull compared to the light that came from the Christmas rose.

The king bent down and held out a bag of gold. "I would gladly trade this," he said, "for a tiny piece of the Christmas rose." And so it came to pass that the king received a piece of the rose, which he planted in the garden outside the palace.

The boy used some of the gold to buy the biggest
Christmas tree in the village, which he and his sister
decorated with ornaments of silver and gold.

Soon their mother was well again, and their father was able to return to work. And the Christmas rose bloomed all year long, sending light and love to every corner of their home.